WILL HOBBS

BEARDREAM

ILLUSTRATED BY JILL KASTNER

ALADDIN PAPERBACKS
New York London Toronto Sydney Singapore

First Aladdin Paperbacks edition June 2000

Text copyright © 1997 by Will Hobbs
Illustrations copyright © 1997 by Jill Kastner

Aladdin Paperbacks
An imprint of Simon & Schuster
Children's Publishing Division
1230 Avenue of the Americas
New York, NY 10020

Also available in an Atheneum Books for Young Readers hardcover edition.
Designed by Michael Nelson
The text for this book was set in Stone Serif.
The illustrations were rendered in oils.
Printed in Hong Kong
10 9 8 7 6 5

The Library of Congress has cataloged the hardcover edition of this book as follows:
Beardream / by Will Hobbs ; illustrated by Jill Kastner.—1st ed.
p.   cm.
Summary: When Short Tail climbs into the mountains to find the Great Bear,
he tires and slips into a dream in which the Great One reveals a marvelous secret.
ISBN 0-689-31973-8 (hc.)
1. Indians of North America—Juvenile fiction. [1. Indians of North America—Fiction.
2. Bears—Fiction. 3. Dreams—Fiction.] I. Kastner, Jill, ill. II. Title. III. Title: Bear dream.
PZ7.H6524Bdn   1997
[E]-dc20
95-36394
ISBN 0-689-83536-1 (Aladdin pbk)

To the Ute children of today and tomorrow
—W. H.

To Rhoda and Renwick

—J. K.

It was springtime in the mountains but the Great Bear was still sleeping. Long after all the other bears had left their dens, he was still dreaming.

In the bear's dream it was springtime and he was fishing in a stream that flowed out of a crystal blue lake. He was catching the trout with his quick paws.

The Great Bear didn't know that he was dreaming.
He thought he was awake, but he was still sleeping.
     Every day the sun rode higher in the sky, but still the
Great Bear didn't wake up. He dreamed he was playing
on the snowbanks, sliding down over and over onto the
green grass. He dreamed he was eating wildflowers, and
they tasted sweet.

In the village below the mountains, a boy everyone called Short Tail was asking around about the Great Bear. Has anyone seen The One Going Around in the Woods? Where is old Honey Paws? Where's Grandfather?

The people began to worry that the Great One had not survived the winter.

Short Tail decided to go up on the mountain to have a look around. The people saw him leave on two feet but soon he was climbing the mountain on all fours, like a bear.

High on the mountain, Short Tail became very tired. He stopped to rest and fell into a dream. In his dream he was kneeling by the entrance of the Great Bear's den. He could hear the bear snoring.

"Wake up, Grandfather," the boy said politely. "You should have been up a long time ago. You'll starve to death."

Still the bear snored on.

"Wake up, Great One!" Short Tail said a little louder.
Only a grunt, and then more snoring.
"Big Tracks, wake up!"
Three quick grunts, and still more snoring.
The fourth time Short Tail yelled with all his might.
"WAKE UP, GRANDFATHER!"

This time the Great Bear came growling out of the den, bristling and terrible, and knocked the boy down. "You woke me up!" the bear snarled, standing over the boy.

"I thought you might need some help. It's spring. It's time for you to come out."

The bear looked all around, blinking his eyes. The wildflowers were already blooming.

"Everyone was afraid something had happened to you, Grandfather."

The Great Bear sat down on his haunches and thought about how respectful this boy was. If the boy had not come he would still be asleep. This boy had come to help him.

"So all this time I've been asleep! Now I've got to hurry! I'll miss it! I might have already missed it!"

Missed what? Short Tail wondered.

"Quick, climb onto my back! For your kindness, I'll show you a secret."

Short Tail clung tight as the Great Bear loped
through the mountain meadows. The sky was
turning dark with night and storm. Into the trees
the bear glided quick as a shadow. The moon was
rising as Short Tail glimpsed the clearing ahead,
where all the bears were dancing.

The bears were dancing in two lines that faced each other, dancing forward and back, forward and back, as thunder rolled and rumbled through the mountains.

"Dance with us," the old bear said, as Short Tail slid from his back. "Dance with us to celebrate the end of winter."

Along with the bears, to the rhythm of the thunder, Short Tail danced, forward and back, forward and back. The bears and the boy danced until the storm passed and the thunder ceased. Then the bears got down on four legs and went their separate ways into the woods.

"Go back and tell the People," the Great Bear told Short Tail. "Show them how to do the bears' dance."

When the boy woke it was night. He was high on
the mountain and he was alone. The moon lit his way
down to the village. When he returned all the people
gathered around, and listened as he told his dream,
and they said he had dreamed a great dream.

Then the people began the first Bear Dance, as the bear had taught them through the dream. Six men sat around a big drum making the thunder as the lines of dancers, the men and the women, faced each other and danced forward and back, forward and back, celebrating the end of winter and the awakening of the bears.

Short Tail was pleased to see all the people dancing.
Someone else was pleased, too. Standing on two legs
just back in the trees was the Great Bear of his dream.
Watching.

It was only for a moment that Short Tail saw him.
As his eyes met the eyes of the bear, the Great One
seemed to nod his head, then returned to all fours and
disappeared into the woods.

AUTHOR'S NOTE

Stories that speak of connections between people and bears have long been a part of the traditions of native peoples. Soon after I came to live in southwestern Colorado, in 1973, I attended the Ute Bear Dance and was moved by the simplicity and power of this ancient rite of spring. As with most oral traditions, there exist variations in the story of the origin of the Bear Dance. *Beardream* is based upon a version of the story common among the Utes of Colorado and Utah. I offer *Beardream* as a tribute to the living tradition of the Bear Dance, in hopes it will never die. It is my belief that future generations of the human family will have greater and greater need for the inspiration of native wisdom, which sees humankind not apart from nature, but as a part of nature.

—Will Hobbs